Let's Go

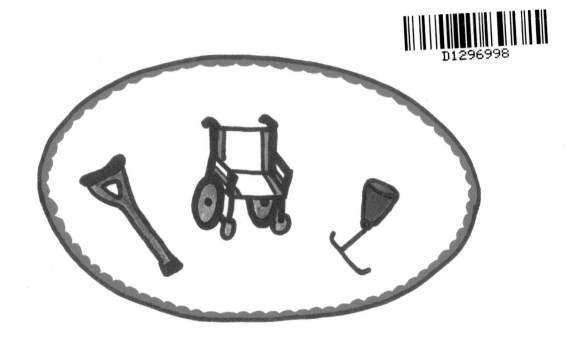

Smile!

Written and illustrated by
Brenda E. Koch

◆ FriesenPress

Suite 300 - 990 Fort St
Victoria, BC, V8V 3K2
Canada

www.friesenpress.com

ISBN
978-1-5255-3976-3 (Hardcover)
978-1-5255-3977-0 (Paperback)
978-1-5255-3978-7 (eBook)

1. JUVENILE FICTION

Distributed to the trade by The Ingram Book Company

This book is dedicated
to all the unique people in the world.

This is ME.

"Prosthetic"
is a big word. It is what
we call something that
replaces a missing part
of your body.

I can do many things
with my prosthetic.

Now,

LET'S GO!

With my prosthetic,

I CAN

walk.

I CAN
RUN.

I CAN

jump.

I CAN

CLIMB.

I CAN

dance,

and
I CAN
play.

Sometimes when I get tired and need a rest, I take off my prosthetic and use a crutch to help me move around the house.

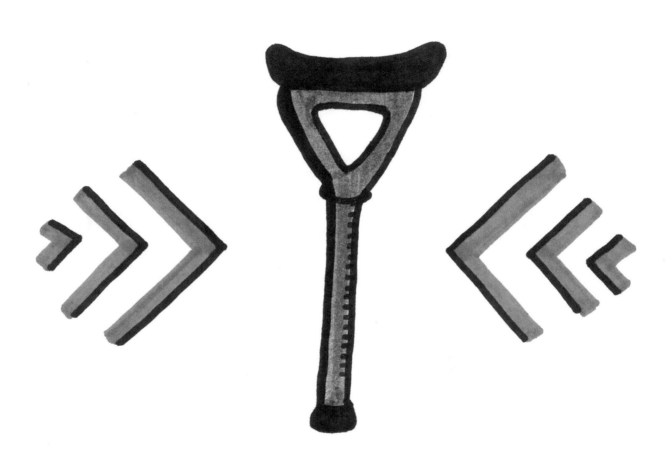

A crutch is an adjustable piece of wood or metal. It has a padded crosspiece for comfort under the armpit. It helps you get from one place to the next.

Sometimes,
when my leg
gets sore from
wearing my prosthetic, or when my
prosthetic needs to be fixed,
I take it off and use
my wheelchair to get around.

A wheelchair
is a chair with wheels on it.
People use one when they
can't walk or just have a
hard time walking.

When, I am in my wheelchair, getting around can be hard sometimes. But many changes are happening in the world that make it easier and safer for me to be a part of my community, and do the things I want to do, no matter how unique I am.

The world is becoming more

"ACCESSIBLE AND INCLUSIVE."

THere aRe TiMes wheN I
waNT TO go iNTO a BUiLdiNg,
BUT I caN'T ...

"Accessible" means that I can get into areas more easily, and without hurting myself, so that I don't miss out on things I want or need to do.

"Inclusive" means that anyone can do things (or at least try them) and go places no matter how different and

SPECIAL
THEY ARE.

I can't climb stairs when
I am in my wheelchair.

But

I can go up a ramp.

It is very hard to open doors when I am in my wheelchair. But most public buildings (like schools or libraries) now have a button on the outside wall beside the door. When I push that button, it makes the door open for me. These doors are wider too, so my wheelchair fits through them more easily.

Most buildings with two or more floors have elevators that will bring me up or down to the level I need.

This is a symbol of accessibility. This sign tells us that certain areas or entries are made accessible for people with needs.

Most public buildings have wheelchair accessible washrooms. They have rails that I can use to pull myself up or lower myself down. These washrooms are for people that need help when they have to use the washroom.

So, when you are going to the washroom in a public building, please remember to choose other washrooms or stalls.

When I am in my wheelchair, and I want to go out into the community, a "Handi-Transit" will pick me up. Handi-Transits are special vans that are built to carry people in wheelchairs.

Hi, I'm Bobby, and I am very happy about all the changes being made to buildings, vehicles, and parks, and even to prosthetics, which are getting better all the time. These changes are making my life easier, and helping me to do things by myself ... and with you.

Now,

About
The Author

Educated as an Aboriginal Child Development Practitioner and Early Childhood Educator, Brenda E. Koch has worked and volunteered with children for over thirty years.

For most of her life, Brenda's mother (who was diagnosed with multiple sclerosis when Brenda was just a little girl) lived in a hospital. During their many visits, Brenda found herself becoming increasingly aware of how people with disabilities are viewed by others. That awareness was the inspiration for this series of books for young children, delving into this sensitive and important subject.

Let's Go! is the second book in the series, following **Let's Play!**, which introduced readers to the concept of people living with disabilities, while celebrating the many ways people are unique, diverse, and the same all at once.

Currently living in Welland, Ontario, Brenda enjoys spending time with her family and friends.

She can often be found swimming at the YMCA and biking with her dog Kilo.

Liked this Book?

Check out Book 1

Let's Play

Written and illustrated by
BreNda E. Koch

YOU'LL LOVE IT!

CPSIA information can be obtained
at www.ICGtesting.com
Printed in the USA
LVHW070839010319
608724LV00002B/1/P